Goings:
In Thirteen Sittings

GORDON LISH
Goings:
In Thirteen Sittings

OR BOOKS
NEW YORK • LONDON

Published by OR Books, New York and London
Visit our website at www.orbooks.com

First printing 2013

Cataloging-in-Publication data is available from the Library of Congress.
A catalog record for this book is available from the British Library.

ISBN 978-1-939293-33-6 paperback
ISBN 978-1-939293-34-3 e-book

Typeset by Lapiz Digital, Chennai, India.
Printed by BookMobile in the U.S. and CPI Books Ltd in the U.K.
The U.S.-printed edition of this book comes on Forest Stewardship Council-certified, 30% recycled paper. The printer, BookMobile, is 100% wind-powered.

TO MARIE-MADELEINE GEKIERE

*Language becomes a compromised ideology,
or else it becomes an idol.
In either case,
we have nothing but trouble.*

—DENIS DONOGHUE

Mother! Father! Please!

—ANON.

CONTENTS

MY PERSONAL MEMOIR

THERE WAS A game we played. Maybe it wasn't a game in and of itself. Is a ball a game? Sure, a ball is not a game. But you can make a game with it, can't you? What can't you make a game with, or of? You just have to decide you are going to do it, is all. Or not even make up your mind and go ahead and decide as such. All you have to do is take the thing and start doing something with it and then say to a boy on the block can you do this and then you show the boy that you yourself can, and then the next thing of it is that that particular boy has to see if he can do it and if he can do it too or even if he can't, well, I ask you, I sit here and in all honesty I ask you, is there or is there not already enough of a game going from just that much of it already, or even better, let's say he can't do it, the boy, that particular boy, then even better, even better if he can't, except who can say, maybe before you know it you're the boy who's sorry you started the whole thing in the first place because maybe the boy we were talking about, maybe he can go ahead and do it better than you can do it and then you wish you had never even taken the reins and

started the game and could instead of any of that instead just stop
playing it but you can't stop playing it, you can't, you can't, because
every time that particular boy on the block comes around he's got
the thing you need for the game with him and he says to you hey
look, can you do this, can you, can you, even if all you have to do is
do it as many times as he can, or do it a little farther than he can, or
do it faster, for instance, than he can, or, well, you know, more times,
more times, or do it some other way different like that.

It was like that when I was a boy.

So the thing itself in the case which I am thinking about, it
was a little red ball—and there was this mysterious way they had
of getting the little red ball stuck to a pretty long red rubber string
and the string, well, it itself was stapled—the string, okay?—yes, yes,
that's exactly the word, stapled, stapled, that's it exactly, this pretty
long red rubber string—it was stapled to a paddle, and so that's the
general thing which I want for you to picture for yourself, the paddle
and the ball and the string—are you with me?—the paddle and the
ball and the string, which the whole idea of the game was for you to
grab the paddle in your hand and see if you could toss the little red
ball up a little bit and then smack it with the paddle and then keep
on smacking it with the paddle until you missed it altogether or,
you know, you just didn't smack it right and it went all crazy in the
wrong direction and then it was the other boy's turn, then it was
his time for his turn, or if there were a lot of other boys, which was
the way it just so happened to be on my particular block, because
on my particular block it was a block with a lot of different boys on

it, it was a block with all sorts of different kinds of boys on it, and yes, yes, don't kid yourself, even at this day and age I could name every one of these various different boys if you dared me to, I could, I really truly could, if you happen to want for us to take the time it would take for me to go ahead and look all of the way back in my mind and name every single last one of them or, okay, okay, maybe if truth be told, maybe I wouldn't be absolutely able to name every last one of them but you can bet your bottom dollar I could probably name plenty enough of them for me to give you the general drift of the thing I am taking the trouble to sit here and tell you about, such as the Stanleys, for instance, such as the Stanleys themselves, for instance, who were, for your personal information, the biggest of all of the boys on the block and who I wouldn't at this particular point in history be the least little bit surprised if they were probably the oldest of all of us too, Stanley R. Florin, for instance, and Stanley S. Baughman, for a second instance, that's right, I'm right, those were the two Stanleys, Stanley R. Florin and Stanley S. Baughman, they were referred to as the Stanleys, or as the two Stanleys, and they were pretty good at the game, let me sit here and tell you that the two Stanleys, that they were pretty goddamn terrific at it, yes indeedy, I am here at this point in history to goddamn tell you the Stanleys were good, the two Stanleys were great, the two Stanleys were the best at the game that anybody at that particular time on the block was, them just going ahead and taking the paddle from you and then smacking the little red ball with it and then just keeping on smacking the crap out of it and then on and on and, wow, holy cow, making the little red ball come whipping right back at the paddle to smack the shit out of it all over again and then smack it some more and keep smacking it some more and, you see, you see, just look at it, are you really trying with your mind to look at it, either of the Stanleys just smacking that little red ball every time the long red rubber string goes snapping out and then comes snapping back at the paddle again—and then again and then again and then this way and then that way until, Jesus, who could stand there and believe it anymore, until you just had to stand there praying and hoping and hoping and praying your turn was never going to come up again but no matter how much you stood there pleading with Jesus Himself, you waiting and waiting and pleading with Jesus please Jesus please don't let it, don't, don't, please don't let my turn come again, please Jesus please, but it would, it would, oh you bet it would, and there you were, standing there with the vicious paddle all ashamed all over again and sad so sad so awful sad from just standing and standing and from hearing yourself screaming out loud to yourself inside of yourself for it all of it to be all over and finished again, please, for it all of it to stop, just stop, just for it to break and be broken, string gone, ball gone, paddle flown out of your hand and for everybody, for all of the boys, for them just to fall over and finally be dead.

Oh, Jesus, your turn!

Oh, Jesus, my turn!

Oh, me, I'm telling you, I myself as a boy, I'm telling you, I'd go ahead and take the handle of it in my hand and go ahead and give the little red ball a little bit of a toss, but try as I might, and I tried, oh brother, oh boy oh boy, did I for Christ's sake try for me to just get the little red ball for it to go up and come back down just even twice for once even if I hit it just as easy as pie just only straight up and right straight back down back to the paddle just twice for once.

But Bobby, there was a boy Bobby, I don't think I told you anything yet about this particular boy Bobby yet—because there was this particular boy Bobby on this block and Bobby was worse.

I'm serious.

I'm being serious with you—there was this Bobby, okay, and believe you me when I tell you, this boy Bobby was worse, this boy Bobby was probably even the worst of all of the boys—until, wait, wait, you didn't hear anywhere near anything yet where the rest of this thing of this is going to come out to its honest-to-God ending yet, you don't even know the first thing of any of the whole unbelievable miracle of this particular story yet, the worst boy on the whole block, the worst, the worst, this Bobby, this Bobby, doesn't the day all of a sudden dawn, doesn't the day all of a sudden come along when this Bobby which I have been mentioning to you, when this particular boy Bobby, he all of a sudden starts taking the paddle and beating the piss out of the little red ball which, like I told you, like I already took the time to tell you, which was stapled to it, just standing there like it was nothing to him if he hit it this way or or if he hit it that way because whichever way this boy Bobby wanted to hit the little red ball he hit it and hit it just the way I just have been

mentioning it to you, the weakest, the littlest, the worst boy on the
block, but wait, wait, what happens but the day fucking dawns,
the day just fucking comes fucking along when, hey, hey, this boy
Bobby, he's taking the paddle and smacking the little red ball better
even than Neal could and better even than Clive could, and you take
Clive, or you take Neal, those two particular boys, they themselves
were almost themselves in a league with either of the two Stanleys,
it's true, it's true, I mean it, I mean it, it just happened just the way I
just sat myself down here and just this minute have been telling you,
this Bobby passing this Clive by and then this Bobby passing this
Neal by and then this Bobby himself almost catching up right there
in front of your eyes to one of the two Stanleys once, this boy on the
block Bobby almost catching up to Stanley S. Baughman once or
with, or to, with the other one of the champs once, to or with good
old Stanley R. Florin once but definitely with or to one or with one
or to one of the other one of them once.

So that's when I had no choice but for me to invent the game
of getting a stick and of hitting a pebble with the stick but not just of
hitting the pebble with the stick but of hitting it right straight at the
face of a boy on the block—and, wait, wait, because I mean hitting
the pebble with all of your might, that's right, hitting it with all of
it, hitting it with absolutely all of it, like every boy who was ever in
his heart a boy who knows things like this right down to his soles
of his shoes, there's this feeling, right, there's this thing you have
to have for you to have a feeling like this, which is this really type
of mysterious type of feeling of it or for it, like of or for you giving

the pebble one of these really great whacks, like whacking it solid in the center of the stick like, I mean like whack, whack, I mean like cracking it right with the right part of the stick, which was just how it was when this particular boy on the block whose name I happen at this particular juncture to think was probably a name like Edwin probably or maybe more like Everett, I think, or like some other terrible name like that, like a name probably beginning with this horrible letter E in front of it, I think, which it is my personal official opinion I have already made fair and ample reference to, but hold it a minute, just hold it for one little more minute, because, yes, yes, Elliot, wasn't it, or spelt Eliot or instead Eliott or something E-name-wise like that?

It put his eye out just the same.

Whichever eye it was, whatever name it was.

He cried a lot with his sight knocked out like that and then he had to go all around all over the block with this drippy-looking bandage hanging half over the whole seepy mess of it and this—me sitting here as God is my judge—this very thing was what this poor particular unfortunate boy had to do for years and years to come, until, thanks to the regular fabulous improvement you can always count on with regards to our modern-day medicine, he got to be old enough and get himself more settled-down in his emotions enough for the experts to go ahead and give him an operation and put a ball of something in there where a real eye used to be for like this fake one to be there in his head instead.

Oh, I know, I know.

Wrong, wrong!—of course I was wrong.

I completely forgot to remember it was Henry—that it wasn't even close to any E-name but that it was a particular name—Henry, Henry!—which I, Gordon, personally hated the guts out of it.

And here's another thing for you to sit there and take into your thoughts in the process of according to them the due consideration due them while you and your family marvel over these long-ago personal events which I, Gordon, am taking the trouble for me to tell you about—that it took two days—*two!*—for the boys on the block to get somebody's mother's broom cut clear away all of the way off from its handle so that, in effect, you had yourself a free-swinging stick which you could really lay your back into and then—wait, wait!—two more days on top of those two days—this crazy thing of this number of *two* again, right, am I right?—the mystery of it, the fucking mystery of it, Jesus, Jesus!—it taking two more days on top of that for us to get the handle sawed off short enough so that you could really stand there and have the presence of mind for you to develop this particular feeling for yourself of getting your feet planted just exactly right enough and really wind that fucking half of a handle up with all of your might and lay your whole young back into it, really get your whole great-feeling boy's back heaved all of the way into it and wing that sonofabitch pebble out there into anybody's face you felt like just like a fucking shot like.

But so what?

I mean, I ask you, did it matter, what did it matter, whose eye you could maybe put out?

I mean, come on, hadn't we all of us already seen what wasn't all of it just only—everything, everything!—just only a different type of a game where there was nothing—nothing!—not anything on all of the whole block which was really on the up-and-up?

FÜR WHOM?

I PLAYED THE piano. Truer to say, I played at the piano or with the piano. Why I am taking pains such as these to wise you up relative to the relative nature of things is to get you informed enough respecting "that relative nature of things" so that you will know, right off the bat, what the score was, piano-wise, music-wise, sister-wise, father-wise, and, most percussively of all, as to all of Miss Bugell. Oh, did I say Dad? Yeah, my dad, my dad. Father. Him too. Or did I in his case neglect to get him prominently enough onto the list of topics? Okay, here we go, nosey as all get-out. We begin by your seeing if you can see my six- and thereafter seven- and eight-year-old behind positioned (in short pants) inches itchily to this side (couldn't help myself, could I?), on the family crewel-work-covered piano bench, of the left-hand (usually but not without certain equally thrilling expectations) hip (indeed, too boney an affair to merit, in the common parlance, the word) and all the better for me for my having, as a child—a six- seven- and eight-year-old child—been, by that age, oh so perfervidly taken with the parts of a female whose "build," as was once the cheeky politeness, gave her to rank rather well in the skinny-to-scanty-styled bodily run-offs, not that such scandalous goings-on ever, so far as I can interpret, did indeed go on in those long-ago arrangements our little narrative endeavor is set in. But tall? Miss Bugell was tall—and from Charlotte, North Carolina, and pasty-looking, or pallid-looking, or perhaps downright pale's the word. Let's face it, plain and pale would do as a pair of excessively generous denotations. The woman was a sight, okay?—and I, Gordon (Gordon!) was mad for her. Well, as you will already have considered, the point of the piano lessons, these conducted weekly in the company of the family baby-grand Knabe, was not so much a matter of all parties suffering for the sake of nurturing an imitation of musicality in the household as it was to situate Gordon's behind within easy reach of his teacher's (you're pushing me, you do recognize that you're pushing me) behind. Too, being Gordon (Gordon!), I was keen to displace my sister in every manner of measurement, and proved so deft at the enterprise that the child (she herself two gross years my senior but still callow enough to fall headlong into rounds of periodic hysterics as she was elbowed well out of the way from any and all lofty touch with the frenzied diurnal exertions in M. Czerny's vicious exercises required of eager tyros in a facsimile of the creative life, practiced ever and ever more feebly among the lesser exigencies: exhibitions of "Chopsticks" and "Hearts and Flowers," occasionally called forth from the uncertain fingers of the convincingly vanquished. So there: an early triumph relished

by the victor so murderously the older child (what *was* her name?)
pulled up stakes in the living room and remanded herself to the
undisciplined custody of her bedroom, to take up, all Bugell-
less, you might say, a stubborn effect to subdue, with flair, the
challenges of number-painting, in oils, portraits of "Lassie" and of
"Bambi" and of "Flicka," proving her still more or less in the arts
game. In brief, I, Gordon (Gordon!) had, in no little while at all,
seen to it that the creature (wasn't it sometimes Natalie, sometimes
Lorraine?) went exiled, without portfolio, to where, I assumed,
that after a quick mucking around with her creative materials
(reviewing her colors), subsided, before supper, into sobful fits
of some unspeakable quality of unslumbrous sleep. Her accruing
humiliations (Natalie's? Lorraine's?) inured to my flourishing
grandiosity in great gobbets of local fame. (Now isn't the boy the
little Orpheus now, such a charmer so impishly in command of
the eighty-eights!) Well, I was Gordon (Gordon!); she, the other
child, less and less often even named. Siblings, families—what
else is there to say? Furthermore (I love that: the chance to flaunt
it with echt balance), it was I whose fingers took up his arpeggios
while his backside thrummed ever more thrummingly to a kind
of low-register attunement to the propinquity of Miss Bugell's
same. Oh, the nearness of her ass (sirs and madam, it was no rump,
now was it?), all yearning angularities not infrequently settling
itself within fractions of centimeters afar. I quote, of course. Yes,
I, Gordon (Gordon!), aged seven, aged six, aged eight, hankered
after that piano teacher as I have never since hankered after the

person of a woman since. Six-foot-four, oh so colorfully colorless, penitentially drab garment hanging pitifully from an immense skeleton afire with the covert thrillings of sexlessness. But hearken, you, this ditty of ours, it shall not (it shan't!) be left to linger any longer, nor any more hygienically (in a Grantland Rice sort of way), on the expectable stirrings radiating from the smelting of an overly praised, normally pathological, achingly competitive kid.

With, beset with—let us call a spade a spade—dreams of pianistic glory at the Knabe and of the vilest carnalings under it, please God those enormously knobby toes of hers, at last liberated from their grim prison footwear, would, while twisting in passion, remain well out of view of the audience seated forever diligently in rapt attendance in my head.

Yes, head—things, matters, what-have-you, they all came, more or less promptly (experience unfolded at a sprint back in those long-ago lassitudinous days), to a head—Natalie, or Lorraine, achieving unimaginable virtuosity on a trumpet she claimed to have pilfered from the school's band-room but which was—this is surmise, to be sure, but an impeccably safe, safely reliable surmise indeed—taken from a cache of mendicant give-aways assembled, pertinent to the holiday season, for an act of discreet late-night trucking to the less fortunate condemned to dwell in the less fortunate town the next town over. But this was nothing, this! Hah!—and hah again! For as concerns my having seized the upper hand hands-down, there came the day when my teacher (the lusciously meager Miss Bugell) imparted to Mr. Lish (he ran things around there, ran them to the fabled faretheewell) her exaxperation with my refusal to play the notes as . . . well . . . as written. "Oh yes," I imagine her having said to this progenitor of mine while the man stood leaning just inside the front door to his house, chest still heaving from the give-you-a-liftless walk home from the train station, good hand gripping the fat sad briefcase he in due course carried into the grave with him, "Gordon's playing has something of a flair, it's to be admitted, yes, but he simply will not bend to the rule of the composer's wishes. Do we understand one another? Perhaps if the girl, your daughter (Natalie was it? Lorraine?) could practice her brass on the school grounds perhaps . . ." fat sad briefcase growing fatter by the instant still gripped in the man's gripping hand, the stately, steely, stentorian Miss Bugell sighing in sympathy and, if it must be told, very ill-concealed impatience.

So that was that.

Love lost, but a version of perversion, as you will see, not long after, gained.

No more improvident renderings of "Für Elise," a squandermania ornamented with unheard-of Gordonesque (Gordonesque!) elements improvised for the love of Gertrude (Miss Bugell's given name, I was to discover when I saw on my father's desk the check that would conclude the fantastical interlude, abandoning crude, mean, joyless boyhood then to be endured Bugell-lessly).

Thump.

A period had come to its period.

Yet in the days, the weeks, the months to come, a new period (of awakening—and of the cruel learning of the infamous lesson of tit-for-tat) came rushingly to the fore.

For now it happened that Dad would, weeknights (and not weeknights), return from his various travails, never without the thunderous briefcase his desperately firm grasp of which would seem to send him wearily listing from one force of gravity to another, drop his burden where he stood, throw an incalculable accounting of exhaustion on the couch (sofa you say?), unlace his shoes, work them off with suffering toes, close his eyes, loosen his necktie, fairly moaning to me, "Sonny boy, your father's darling sonny boy, sit, please, and please play for your father, cutie boy— that thing, that thing the *mieskeit* was going crazy to teach you, the Beethoven which makes the Brahms look sick."

Taking, in the tenderest (nay, most dramatic) fashion, my place at the centerpiece of our living-room décor, I would manage to produce a soulful simulacrum of the identifying bits hinting at the opening flourishes of Beethoven's "Für Elise"; shortly thereafter, on detecting Dad's heroically stertuous breathing, in merest moments, overtaking my musicianship, I would, cheered with a lifetime's chance to put the full panoply of my genius on parade, fall to swaying with the rising emotion issuing into all the parts of my uncontainably responsive person at the first signs of proof in witness of Gordon's (Gordon's!) inspired revisions of Brahms' feloniously overrated rival in this puerile contending for mastery status in the Germanic mode.

My father would, thank the heavens, sleep, rest, curl into himself in the effort to regain his dignity, while I, Gordon (Gordon!), his beloved muse, would thereupon let fly with everything I had. "Can't that stuck-up brat be made to shut up in there!" Natalie, or Lorraine, would yell from the kitchen, cueing my mother (Mother!) to call out, in pained affirmation, "Gordino, dear child, *pianissimo, pianissimo*, have mercy on us, have mercy, God Himself beseeches you, please!" Me, I'd scream back, this between brilliantly berserk runs from one end of the Knabe to the other, "But can't you people tell Father needs his sleep?"

Natalie, or Lorraine, she'd show up in the living room after enough of these refrains, blow a hellish blast of her trumpet-like hand-me-down into the poor devil's ear, and at that, as they declared, I imagined, in all the better households on the block, dinner was served.

Well, where I, in the opposition, dwelt, the occasion was referred to as "supper," enough said? After which exercise in civilizing ourselves, the authentic brat in the family would repair to her room for homework and rearranging the demography of her dolls, Mother (Mother!) would take to bed with a migraine and to, nevertheless, a marathon of all-night mending or, more latterly in our family's history, sewing and gluing glittery beads and spangles onto, what seemed to me, a perfectly presentable collection of handbags, reticules, purses, clutches, and those big wooden-handled carry-alls the ladies who crocheted, knitted, and embroidered carried.

Dad (Father!) would return to the couch, flutter the evening's newspaper for sufficient effect, and then, finished with the seriousness of the world, utz me piano-ward, cooing to me, "Sonny boy, softly, softly—please again, again, be a sweetheart, sweetheart, and serenade your father who adores you with that wonderful, please, you know, Beethoven piece." I would.

Of course, I would.

Forever I would.

To this day, just days from age eighty, how I wish and how I wish I could, that I could.

He'd sleep.

Or seem to.

Then, eyes fast shut, thick hairy hand lifted to the ceiling in an act of death-prone importuning, wave me over to him there on the couch, make just enough room for me, then curve me bodily into his chest, his neck, his arms, his thighs, knees, legs, belly, groin, and, truly sleeping, or truly struggling to seem to be sleeping, take up either of my hands and, in time with his gentle rhythmic breathing, dig, with a dark ragged forenail, dig deep, and more deeply, again, again, into the skin, down into the flesh, one by one into the backs of the forgiving agony of his sonny boy's virtuosic (mmm, how shall we say this?) fingers.

My father.

His son.

Gordon.

(That's right—just like a family, all in all.)

AVANT LA LETTRE

THE TITLE, PAY it no mind. It does not apply. It does not appertain. I appended it strictly for pretention's sake—also, for alliteration's, or is it assonance's? You would think, that for *that* sake, or, anyway, for those, I'd mooch on over to the dictionary to look to see what it's all about, but I have aged past the stage when willing to submit myself to the care of the lexicographical community. Moreover (don't you love it, *moreover?*), I, Gordon (Gordon!), don't know shit of the lingo the title is empedestaled in. So where, then, did I, Gordon (Gordon!), get the thing from?

Beats me.

Sat myself down to tell you about a mystery (the vanishing of the man on the corner), and, lo, the title ("Avant la Lettre") just more or less popped into my (into Gordon's!), ah, let us say, frame of attention, still assonantially—or is it morphologically?—speaking.

Unless it's morphemically I should have, or should have ought to have, said.

All this was—the foregoing, that is, or *that was*—moreoverly spoken.

So what, it is wondered, popped into yours (head, frame of attention—Jesus, nay, consciousness, oh my Christ!) in the course of your making your way from up there, where a pompified affiliation was claimed, to down here, where, get set, it's in two seconds going to be pretty safely solid fare, a totally meat-and-potatoes rendering of the menu, bowls of nutriment fit for the most unforgiving of tables?

I bet plenty.

Or, better still, nothing, not a jot of the associational (tell Sartre, just to begin with) at all.

So here we go—here comes the original play of the hitherto initial conditions—written (indited?) back before the occurrence of the poppitudinous event which I, Gordon (Gordon!), instants ago, just, you know, diktat-wise, mentioned to you.

You ready?

Because not all of the parties franchised to vote are yet agreed to the giving of an account of the long and the short of the matter hinted at (tell Barthes, tell Derrida, tell Badiou) in the title determined for this publication. Yes indeed, it's, to be sure, the fruit vendor I, Gordon (Gordon!), am talking about—unless, now that such lengthsome time has elapsed, the version in your hands (tell Buber, tell Levinas, tell Harold, if you will, Bloom) is heading instead elsewhere, or elsewhere instead—careening, namely, for the Man on the Corner, providing one does not more popularly—or say I said *conventionally*—write "at," this more aptly expressed, say, by shifting to, or by undertaking a shift to, italics—thus, or thusly: *at.* But we need not linger on the distinction (what distinction, who sees the least evidence of one stinking spicule of distinction?), save to observe that he, the fruit vendor, or appositely, the man on, or at, the corner, despite the bearing implied by the occupation explied, might (who the dickens has descried a datum otherwise?) have appreciated these various and sundry refinements in discourse— which, in the latest fashion, is to say: "the conversation." Take it from me, Gordon (Gordon!), that whatever species of menace the man's presence in our district posed, it must not be concluded the chap was lacking an education in the pickier formalities once the face and buttress of our language. To be sure, the fruit vendor seemed to me (you know whom) more a refugee from retail sales in exotic woolens (or is it *woollens*?) than toil in some expression of manual labor, albeit one not necessarily experienced in the hands-on kind. In another place, at another time (tell Trilling, go ahead and try to tell the snot—or is it instead your churlish practice to favor "try *and* tell"?), you could have thought this parvenu a miscreant in recovery from the medical arts or even an adventurer erstwhilishly exiled from the ultra-high sciences. But my sense (*Gordon's* sense!) of the fellow's history—when he, the very immigrant and his foodstuffs (this latter a klaxon of sonorous gaiety heaped into a harlinquinade of glistering comestibles borne gaudily aloft as raked—or is it banked?—levels of sylvan color sheltered ever so genially under a foursome of the palest blue *cum* faintly lavender pin-striped umbrellas superintended in the dispensation of their arrangement for to exact from the cannily misted perishables on such vivacious display beneath them the effect of a fairyland copia of abundance—excess, excess, pleonasm, pleonasm, redundancy, extraneity, the tautology of attraction—or the lure, the allure, of a trap, a trap?) appeared among us—was rather darker, you may tentatively certainly say, than the facts. Not that . . . not that . . . oh, please, please—feel free to finish, in suitable pursuit, with an adverbial subordinate clause of your (do, also, take note of the refuseniky absence of the possessively adjectival particle "own" reflexively hooked illegitimately illogically virtually universally parasitically vulgarianly prefatorally to some abused host of a nominative) minting.

But how to adduce facts?

There were (the facts, the facts—hey, are you, synthesizing-wise, making the merest effort at all?), and will remain, unknown to the lot of us, although much (though not—not by miles, not by leagues, not be measures galore—nearly enough) was revealed at the inquest arising out of the *what*, the *what*?

Well, why not the street merchant's "elimination" (in order that some instance of enthusiasm be solicited on your part)? Say I said "the death" of the street (actually, that of the sidewalk, *ness paw*?) merchant.

But all seriousness, just between you and me—honestly, honestly—can you believe it?

The demise of an appellation?

Well, name it and (tell Schopenhauer, tell Schelling, tell Spinoza or Freud) it dies.

Had one ever visited with the chap, passed the time of day with the chap, exchanged with this personage comments on the proverbial cabbage, for one, or, for two, the proverbial king? No, no, no, no—one had, in sum, indicated what was wanted, paid out currency (bills, coins, tendresse) from one's pocket for one's purchases, taken the sack ensacking these specifications, and, hastily, pushed on, or back, thank the gods, for home.

That's it.

Apart from the coinciding of the big hellos.

HELLO.

Buyer's, seller's, each a hand held high a good half block distant.

HELLO.

In whole-hearted greeting.

The fellow's big foreign teeth agleam with, or agleam in, welcome—either with or in anticipation; either with or in an apprehension of the commission of an act of commerce in the offing.

Sublime.

Nah, forget it—fuck it!

I can't, I just can't—and I'm sorry, I'm sorry.

Skip it—*no can do.*

Keep keeping this pointillage up.

Where's in me anymore (in Gordon, in *Gordon!*) the discipline for the creation of the succession of elaborations, for the concatenation of the falsifications, for the accruing of the exhausting collocations?

I'm sad.

Plus: all-out, plumb-in—emptied, Jackson, *emptied*!—of whatever it takes.

You understand me.

Writing's not the god of me.

Corruption is.

Not that it's a tittle different for any of us.

Listen, I, Gordon (Gordon!), am crapping out from cancer of the waist.

Tell Seneca.

Tell Longinus.

Tell Young Doctor Malone, Old Doctor Zorba, and, for symmetry's sake, Dr. Christian's sidekick, performed ever so thrillingly by Rosemary DeCamp.

So which is it, then—*dying of* or *dying from*?

Oh, one more thing, a postscriptum, eh what?

The Doorman's Tale:

"Where's he gone to?"

"Who?" says the doorman.

I says to the doorman, "Are you fucking with me? Don't you dare fuck with me. The fruit guy at the end of the block—where'd he go, didn't you see?"

Says the doorman to me, "Ill-phrased, Mr. Lish—rightly considered in the light of Kristeva's commonplace—'The speaking subject gives herself away.'"

"You bum," says I.

"Besides which," yon doorman says, preparing himself to misquote Lingis, "what is it, this imperative we suffer to perceive? What price," the bastardo leans into me and cheekily, cheekily murmurs, "impercipience?"

Mark you my words, Gordon's (Gordon's), isn't this how our malignancies are rumored to gain the upper hand?

And that, buddy-boy—that, for your information, that was just your on-duty doorman.

Or—hyphenlessly—your doorman on duty.

SPEAKAGE

I SAID, "WHAT is it, die?"

She said, "Who said such a thing?"

I said, "What does it mean, somebody dies?"

She said, "Never you mind, a child!"

I said, "Is it bad? Then it's bad."

She said, "What kind of child speaks to his mother like this?"

I said, "You can tell me."

She said, "Tell you, tell you—all of a sudden such words."

I said, "Then it's bad, isn't it?"

She said, "Listen to this talk from a kidlach. Be quiet. Go to sleep."

I said, "I can't til you tell me."

She said, "I'm your mother and I told you."

I said, "Are you trying to scare me?" I said, "You're scaring me."

She said, "To speak like this, for shame."

I said, "Do I die?"

She said, "You want to make your mother sick?"

I said, "So you know, don't you?"

She said, "What know, where know?"

I said, "Am I going to die?"

She said, "Please, the language of it. Sleep."

I said, "Who dies?"

She said, "Maybe sometimes certain people, yes."

I said, "Not everybody?"

She said, "Who is everybody?"

I said, "You, for instance—do you die?"

"Please," she said. "Shush," she said.

"Then it's true," I said.

"Enough," she said. "Sleep," she said.

I said, "Sleep? There is no sleep," I said.

"So fine," she said, "a person dies."

I said, "People, then? All of the people?"

She said, "People, what people?—it's nothing, people."

I said, "You mean everybody really?"

"Please," my mother said. "Just sleep," my mother said.

I said, "You mean you too—that you're going to die too?"

"Who doesn't die?" my mother said. "To live is to die," my mother said.

I said, "Yes, yes," I said. I said, "That's you," I said. I said, "But what about me?"

IN THE DISTRICT, INTO THE BARGAIN

HERE'S A BIT for you. It's an impressive one too. My bet is you are going to be really refreshingly impressed with it, or by it, which I have to tell you is what I myself was when the woman involved in the event disclosed her heart to me. First, as to setting—temporal, spatial, all that. So, fine, so the thing starts maybe all of an hour ago just a block from where I am sitting right this minute typing this up for you to read it and get out of it the same kick I did. She types too—the woman. She is always typing, is my understanding—or was, back when I used to see her somewhat, let us just fancy, social-wise. As a matter of fact, when I said to her, "What's up? I mean what are you doing here in this neighborhood? Do you have a pass, were you issued a pass, a license maybe, any kind of a permit you can show me authorizing you to come up here into this restricted district of mine?" she laughed. I think she thought I was trying to be funny. Let me tell you something—that's the one thing I never try to be—namely, funny. No, no, I was just doing what I could to maybe get away with having to snoggle for the usual sort of talk, lay on her a smart-aleck greeting of a sort, which apposition I only went to the bother of just now constructing so I could say sort and sorts, repeating and repeating stuff to stuff the insidious silence with insidious sound, however otiose or bootless or inutile dexterity appears (to be?) *on the surface.* You get what I'm getting at?—the stressing of the effect of there being something sly down beneath down under things as regards below the surface, see? But which surface, eh wot? Or, anyway, surface of exactly what, eh wot? (You see? Can't help myself. It's like this thing I've got which is like an irresistibly compulsive thing.) Oh, boy, I am all of a sudden so tired. I, Gordon, son of Reggie, am all of a sudden so suddenly utterly all in, just fucking pooped. Like, you know, like weary, wearied, *ausgespielt* if you're German, right? Nap. But, hey, before I fall and hit my head, I'm just going to go ahead and take myself a little teensy tiny nap, fair enough? Be back in a shake, I promise.

Mmm, nice. Told you I'd be right back. So there. Good as my word. Plus, feeling ten thousand percent. Nothing like sleep, let me tell you. Anyway, as I was going to say to you, small talk, the ceremonial, it gets me jumpy and tongue-tied, see?—especially when there's the blam of a city smashing the nuclei of your cochlea from all four sides of your brain. Or, okay, six. I mean, the street. Knocking yourself out to make a show of confecting coherent conversation on the street, okay? This was the street. Or, fine, on the street. Or *in* it—since as for *on*, we were, the scene was taking place, the one consisting in this woman and I—*on* the sidewalk. But I may have already said so, mayn't I have? Anyway, I was aiming for home from marketing and here she was, the woman I am telling you about, making her way along the sidewalk, coming right dead-on at me, a woman I, Gordon, had not, I swear to you, laid eyes on in a shockingly long time. Some beauty too. A real knockout. But in her years, of course, not in the slightest other than I. That's right—we're old. Okay, so this woman laughs a little and she says to me, "I was at the school—went by for a used-book sale at the school." "Really?" I say. "At the school, you say? Buy anything?" I say. "Oh, just these," she says, spreading open the dainty shopping bag she's hauling with her and giving me a peek inside. There's two books in there. I finger them around, trying to get it to look as if I'm earnestly interested in getting a look, and see, yeah, yeah, just crap, more crap, writing, writing, etc. and so on. "Sophie, this is crap," I says to her, and she says, abashed is the word, or embarrassed, "I know, I know." So I says to her, "Sophie, will you please explain yourself? I am waiting to hear you make a forceful enough attempt to explain yourself," which, you know, gets another laugh out of her, but she touches my arm, the way you do, and I do ditto to hers, and this part of it is really honestly terrific for me because, don't make me have to say it to you again, this person is, old as she is, a really terrifically classy-type of a looker. "And you?" she says, "because I never see you on the street anymore—oh, but probably it's me—always hatching up dreams at home by reason of beating my keyboard to death."

"Um, not me," I say. "Quit it all just after the wife died. It's not for me anymore, all of that maddening shit, verbs and nouns and worse. What I do," I says to her, "is I keep myself frantically busy fussing with the place."

"Is that so?" the woman, tired and tiresomely, says.

"Seems to be," I say, and can see this powwow half a lick from a ghastly stall, and, thus, high time for everybody's sake to make all speed for a semi-graceful goodbye and let us please get going on our separate ways.

I touch her arm.

It's nice. Like sleep.

"Got to giddyap," I say. "Projects."

"Oh?" she says. "Like what?" she says.

Well, you can see how it is—one, I don't want to be outdone, take off with the question, with *her* question, still in charge of the verbal situation which had been developing on the street just more or less just moments ago, which would be, if I did it, did yield, did give way, did fail to return reply, it would be like my giving this person the, you know, the victory, you might not inappropriately say, yes—and, two—two, I all of a sudden figure there's maybe more to be said for touching hastening on the way in the offing for me here, so sexily, you might say, I says to the woman, "Ah, you know, just puttering around with my place, keeping things up to grade—or is it code?—doing what I can so the wife does not have to rest in everlasting shame."

"Barbara?" the woman says.

"That's right," I say. "Good of you to remember the name. And Howard?" hoping and praying it's me who's this time remembering right (unless it's aright), that it's not John or something, Alphonse or Gray. "Pretty tough still, is it, or are you actually getting yourself settled in with all of the adjustments and all?"

"Yes, Howard," she says, and looks off up into the wild blue yonder and, still gazing away, says to me, "Projects you said? Such as what?" she says to me, saying to me, after her saying just that little bit to me, not one other word, not nought, by Christ—until I, Gordon, am standing there with her on the sidewalk with her all talked-out, not having shown this person up, I should certainly say, not having exhibited to this person just what fucking grief is all about, which is when the woman gives me a look and says to me, touching my arm again *into the bargain*, "Oh, Gordon, you are such a tease," and keeps touching my arm, keeps her hand in noticeably secure touch with my arm, in the manner of somebody determined to hold a person stationed right there where the two of them, persons the pair of them, are—as in don't leave, don't leave, and, sighing, saying to me, she says to me, "I know, I know—it's exactly the same with me." And here it happens, I can tell it, I can tell it, this woman is going to come at me with a comeback, goddamnit—I took too stuporously long trying to think up some sort of a reportable project—the mattress, the bedskirt, the phone in the kitchen sticky with its locale in the vicinity of lots of lonely frying.

But it's crazy how I remember it.

His pipe. The man's pipe. Her husband's pipe, which I, Gordon, first apprehends as a pipe, as just a fucking pipe, as just the prop like a man named Howard, isn't it, type of chap for him to sport, a pipe, hah!

"Oh," she murmurs to me getting herself right in close to my face, "but isn't one forever thinking of it—Howard's favorite pipe?"

Me, I told her about some stuff I couldn't seem to shut up about—the mattress, the bedskirt, the kitchen telephone. "Oh," she says, "isn't it what always so heartbreakingly happens when you don't buy bedding at a department store where if you don't, then you don't have any, not the least, latitude as to any recourse of return, or last resort to it, or for credit? Gordon," the woman says to me, admonishing me, and not at all soothingly, "don't tell me Barbara never advised you to keep yourself well out of the reach of the specialty shops!"

I think I said, "Latitude?"

I think I may have said, "Latitude?"

You can lose the thread, you know.

You can lose it even if it's your own textile you're weaving.

Jesus, I am so goddamn tired again. Oh, man, am I . . . beat! Do you ever get to feel like this? You know what I mean? But maybe you don't. Maybe you're different from me. But maybe you're not like her, either. I mean, I'm thinking a pipe pipe—like a briar pipe, right? But you know what in just mere minutes from then I'm willing to grant? And, hey, listen, I'm prepared to insist it's a sign of growth in me, isn't it?—this recent willingness I just mentioned to you where I'm willing to grant somebody a little something by way of exoneration—as in maybe a little benefit of the doubt.

"Sophie," I says to her, tap-tapping the handier of her elbows with my two happy fingers working in synchrony. Still, doing this pretty consolingly, you do, I trust, understand—tap, tap, tap, gently, gently. I says to her, "Sophie, do you actually mean for me to interpret your meaning as meaning like a pipe in the basement or something—not something like a Meerschaum, right? But, you know, instead—instead an overhead pipe, industrial and all that?"

"Well," she says (Sophie says to me, Gordon, you do continue to see), "dear Howard, dearest Howard, he had, I have to tell you, the man had picked out a big green heating pipe he felt very protective about."

Or of, I, for the record, corrected—but, uncharacteristically, keeping my annoyance to myself.

Fuck it. You probably know how it goes from here—her getting me, with a touch and a half, to go with her over to her place to see it down there in her building's basement—some superintendent's gardener's glossy high-class green. Then I, of course, got her to come hurry right over with me to my place and, you guessed it, showed her, I showed her, absolutely—well, yes— every dazzling detail.

Which is to say the sole project left to me.

Oh hell, the one, to be fair, left to the legion of both of us, I suppose it's, inescapably, only virtuous for me to allow.

VIEW FROM THE OTHER SIDE

YOU LAST BEHELD the Fifty-ninth Street Bridge in this or the antecedent century? Unless it's called the Queensborough now. Who can tell anymore? It's been millineries and chin straps and millineries galore. Listen, what hasn't been? They could have revisionated the name of it and uninformed the newspapers. This is one of the projects they historically execute—slip on a different name for it and keep it secret until the next stage. It happens to be Perchik in a nutshell and history as well. Things are all of them akin to progress, only inorganic from the word go. Besides, what kind of a mental case dares decline custard? We'll come again to consider again when Medicare merges with Christianity. But who cares? Do I care? Look, you want me to tell you what I want? A fork on the tray, Perchik seizing it and mortally stabbing me with it before the peaches are peeled and served. Think about it. Misapplication. The man could merely maim me. When did I, one of the earliest devotees of humanity, not consent to my being maimed by a maniac? Let's face it, what's the story of the spread?

There is no going back, is there? Motion has gone to the dogs as a concept. Listen, I myself was the sole possessor of a semi-mild condition. That's official. As to the question of you personally, so? I mean, all my life that's all I've ever been—all fucking ears, okay? Guess who's getting a polyurethane utensil in the eye if he keeps on confusitating my "food." Is there one thing I am not, as an American, convinced of? Cultivate the utilization of A CERTAIN TYPE OF LANGUAGE and the next thing you know, the whole United States nation has to go ahead and take another one in the chops for the sake of socialization. People. Don't they make you sick? Perchik says, "Grow up. Act your age." Fine. Between you, me, and the lamppost, Updike's not his name. You know what shuts everybody up? That does. Okay, let's switch topics. What say ought be proposed apropos of the Fifty-ninth Street Bridge? Is the reason why you're having a tough time following me the same as the reason why you're having a tough time following yourself? Here's some factuality for you—it isn't even a real bridge in anything close to the biblical sense. I looked it up. I'm telling you, I, Gordo, took it upon myself to exercise the initiative to inquire into the subject from a materially theoretical aperçu. You know the George Washington Bridge, the Verrazano Bridge, the Bridge of Sighs? Those are bridges. They're like for people not just to get across over to the other side of something by, they're for people to—skip it, sentence was already a pain in the ass miles before it had its toe in. It's an affiliation, you do realize. Trust me, I used to teach contrivance. It's college-level thinking, granted—whereas Paley and Barthelme, they were, or weren't, an

item in your better class of sexual magazine? Sneeze if you must.
With regard to our republic, what used to be totally lacking in it
still is. Whither refinement? Why is this so hard for everybody
to understand? Abominable as Perchik is, is he nevertheless not
perfectly pervious? Time was when I was pretty impervious, too.
This is what this issue is. Take any edition of *The Antoich Review*.
Now tell me who Robert Fogarty is. Don't make me laugh. You know
what's a crying shame? The whole affair—it's indecent. Turning to
our study of the infrastructure, doesn't it look like shit from here?
From coast to coast, you know what? The pressure is fantastic. The
only explanation is this—Gordo's got a certain something on a
certain editor-in-chief. See the hyphens? Believe you me, they're
a thorn in the man's *kishkes*. Ha ha ha ha ha ha ha. That's a set of
seven—the acoustical limit, breathingly speaking. I'm going to tell
you one last thing—never mock Queens. You know what I miss?
I miss seeing derricks. I miss seeing kids who knew how to hold a
pencil right. But that's it. Being in here, not one other thing I can
think of would I adjudge myself unjustly deprived of—except, of
course, something smart to read. Also Perchik's wife's keester,
which was, as the keesters of wives who shlepped upstate to visit
went, ingenious. Oh well, the lady's probably been renamed by now.
Calling herself, or being called, Nina Foch. Or maybe Faye Bainter of
yesteryear. Check the tray for a fork first. Perchik suffered. Do I hear
a rebuttal? But that's Perchik. Now take a taste of tonight's pudding.
It is or isn't underwritten by the United Federation of Teachers?
Canned peaches by Krupp—sure, sure, I get it, how impeccably

politically convenient. Time was when what? Time was when the human race spoke English! Watch Fogarty—if only to begin with. Not to mention the Department of Transportation and its dirty stinking lousy rotten vendetta against free speech.

GNAT

SHE SAID, "PUT it on, I want to see it on you." Or "see you in it." She perhaps said "in it," and not "on you," but in either event I complied, got into the shirt that I had purchased, what does one say, on the fly? By gum, yes, there had not been any of this frantic shopping around, that I can promise you, trying store after store, nor, when the saleslady had pointed it out to me, did I find myself the least uncertain, asking, as a person unsure of himself might, "Looks good, you bet—but what else do you want to show me? I mean, don't you think you should show me something apart from just this?"

No, I took my purchase as one would take to oneself a kidnapped newborn, paid for it, and left the premises, assured by the, what do they say for this occasion nowadays, not saleslady but server, that the shirt needed only be washed and then let hang to dry for it to be restored back to its original good looks.

Oh, the relief, the relief, to have proved myself already poised on the farther end of the accomplishment of an initial gesture toward a bold review of the long-postponed project respecting the lightening of my hourly, my daily, my lifely load: cut down on the ironing, shift footwear into sneakers from shoes, and then, refreshed, encouraged, stimulated by this hurtling into assertive action, press on from there with the embrace of synthetic fabrics, the time-honored ones demanding more and more labor for me to get about in, as my strength—I am no spring chicken anymore, it might interest you to learn—is ebbing, waning, suit yourself, choose a word. This, then, creaking in my jeans, as it were, was the measure by which I was charting the rate, and the most recently achieved stage, of my ageing: to wit, the increasing burden to my body clothes were. So I was resolved to quit heaving my person around in cottons and woolens, for example, and to get ready to consent to the genius of micro-fiber, a feathery, gleaming, watertight substitute for the materials God had all too rashly proffered to us in their place. The shirt—a much-pocketed affair with a stunning variety of Velcro fastenings shrewdly featured here and there—would establish me as someone who had taken a first earnest step toward adjusting himself to inevitable defeat in his struggle against the superior tactics in reach of the relentless—why pussyfoot around?—malicious forces in charge of the earth, a longish, not unchallenging bit of prose, that, don't you think, at least for one whose energies are in such quick-footed retreat.

She said, "Put it on."

I held it up to my chest and smiled, the modesty incumbent upon the unconquerable.

She said, "No, put it on. I want to see how it fits."

"It fits," I said. "I'm positive of it."

She adopted an expression not as forgiving as the one that had received me when I had returned home, my not undifficult mission completed.

"You mean," she said, "you didn't try it on?" She said, "Are you telling me you walked out of that shop without seeing what the thing looked like on you?" She said, "Darling, you are definitely not standing there telling me that, are you?"

But I was.

For it was true.

I said, "The tag says there's an insecticide somehow suffused in the material." I said, "It says it wards off mosquitoes, even kills them."

"Put it on," she said.

I put it on.

"Come closer," she said.

I did as she said, and before I could defend myself, she knocked my elbow out of the way and hooked her finger—from outside the shirt, from *outside*—through into the armpit.

And wiggled it.

The finger.

"What's this?" she said.

"What's what?" I said.

"This," she said.

"What?" I said, wondering, but not all that assiduously, how she had managed to get her finger into my armpit from the outside.

From outside the shirt, I mean.

"This slit," she said. She said, "What's this doing here? Not that I want for us to overlook this one on the other side over here. Are these gills?" she said. She said, "Are you actually wearing a shirt with gills?"

Well, it turned out I was.

Holes.

One supposes to vouchsafe upper-body ventilation for the active man.

"Take it back," she said. "Get your money back," she said.

I took it back. Demanded a full refund. Explained I had taken it for granted that shirts were still made the old foolish way, that I was very sorry for my hurried though admittedly enfeebled assumption, might I please have refunded to me what I paid for it.

There was some grumbling, of course. I think a somewhat ungentle remark might have been passed, somewhere at a little distance from me, to the effect that the elderly ought not to be released into an engagement with citywide retail commerce without a guardian present. There's only this left to say—that as the paperwork was being enacted, I accommodatingly burbling something about how admirably clean I'd kept the shirt, that I had not even tried it on in front of the mirror or, ah God, my wife, that as I was doing what I could to distract the sentinels posted at the door of the new epoch from their calculating the full moral cost of their vexing themselves with my case, I noticed a blackish blot on the shirt's placket and, reflexively, stupidly, for wouldn't this surely give me away, I darted my hand out to obscure the evidence of my felony.

But not fast enough.

Not for the fellow processing the refund.

He beat me to it, the sharpster—plucked (from the placket; yes, I would say placket again if I were less alert to the finer if superficial aspects of this confession than I guess you reckon me to be) plucked the blot off the shirt and flicked it—magic, magic!—away.

Weeks later, napping, only just yesterday, as a matter of fact, in the course of an ingenious digression erupting during an especially vapid dream, I came, all at once, to recognize what the salesman—whoops, the server, right?—had snapped behind his waist forever off into the abyss, this without the slightest indication of a hiatus appearing in his otherwise superbly confident dealing with one of the untold bothers of the mercantile day.

So it worked!

By Jupiter, these modern times, what will they have the cheek to pull on us next?

As for her?

She's okay—except she's yet to quit mentioning her intention to pick up a couple of frog-resistant skirts, snickering hideously just as her tongue curls into the cusp of what seemed to me to be precipitating the utterance of a nonlatinate near-rhyme.

KNOWLEDGE

I DO NOT have to do this, you know. It is not mandated by government, you know. Nothing forces me to say what I will—or shall!—you know. It is, rather, my means of giving back to "the" community, of one's seeking to perform usefully, even munificently, in the—well—in the modest manner that might, on occasion, by a dues-paying member of mankind, be accomplished.

Like the alliteration I just indulged myself in.

I mean (heh-heh, see?), I could have gone farther, or further, mounting a montage of even more ems, or, if you insist, em's.

Dub it my bearing, my engaging existence at what is judged to be a depth deep enough but not so sheer that ostentation ensues. To be sure, taking the flyer down, as I had just done in the course of my stroll back (in return, as in effectuating a ritornello) from the bakery, ripping the big sheet of paper from where it had been plastered to the lamppost, made me a degree uneasy on this score.

Was the deed too showy?

What were the chances I was being observed?

I do not believe neighbors—residents of my building, that is; tenants, that is, legitimated denizens enjoying the privileges of tenancy herein—saw me at it: to wit, my exerting no little effort to rid the streetscape of the big sheet of paper without my rending it into pieces, and then (failing at this, failing not thoroughly but discoverably clownishly at this) to remove the duct tape that was wound around the topmost and bottommost margins of the thing, tethering the whole of it—a poster, a poster!—to the lamppost with, as the poet has proposed, a vengeance.

Yes, perfect, perfect!—that's the fashion to express it—vengeance, vengeance—vindictively.

The bastards.

Oh, I imagine the doorman must have caught me at it, mustn't he? For he was there when I, not many strides from home, maneuvered to aim myself toward him, this worthy's massive hand on the brass-work, the whole of him at the ready to see to it that his master's motion not be made tardive as I glided past the good fellow into the lobby and thus into the warmed air thereinward, gaining ground ever so fluidly onwards and, thereafterwards, whilst awaiting the arrival of the elevator, calling out to the chap, perhaps a dot too cheerily, "Ferdy, have I greeted you on this merry Flag Day of ours? If not, then to you, Ferdy, I say let this day be savored as the merriest of them—i.e., Flag Days—ever, that is!"

Alas, the cunning son-of-a-bitch must have seen me at it.

Jesus Christ, what now?

Too late, too late!—the big sheet of paper crushed into parts—hidden, hooray, successfully hidden!—squeezed, as the ghastly shreds were, down into the crease of my coat pocket, a grand patch-pockety affair commodious to a fault. Whereas to the other side of myself, employing no more than the chilled tips of my fingers, I held aloft, ever so deftly, the loop of the sack in which were composed the bran muffins I had gone to collect from the pastry shop so popular in this particular (hmm, par*ti*cular) precinct of ours.

Wretchedly sorry.

Did it again—the pee's repeated.

Really, it is the awfulest tic, I do actually quite admit it.

Oh, how not concede that sometimes—nay, "oftentimes, oftentimes"—(as the crude, as the untutored, as the reader cannot yourself but have noted, have lately taken to saying)—if, if, if there is to be parsed the natural policy of this reported reflex of mine, this, you do see, from the lowlier view, there is thereby to be beheld, it is granted, a practice vicious, murderous—for the sake of the effect (*i.e.*, for effect's sake)—or (sake be cursed!) for worse?

At all events, I am restored to my habitation now: bran muffins, not yet unpacked, resting in their sack on the kitchen table, I seated (or situated) on this frail stool, inscribing for your entertainment the day's prescribed confession, concession, you—this is the United States of America!—choose.

For this is what this is.

And so forth and so on.

Did I, Gordon Lish, have anything to do with the matter mentioned on the flyer? Or, then, call it "public notice," if you wish.

Rhyme, rogue, rhyme—hah!

(Not entirely, isn't it, un-akin to "ah-hah"?)

The very thought, the very idea, the very thing of such a thing—willikers!

Let us first recognize that it has been years since the era when I was other than a mere pedestrian. The "public notice," howsoever, if you *still* will, appertains to a "motorcycle accident," does it not? By Jupiter, dearest forerunners in the celestial circle—a motorcycle accident, oooo, *brrr*.

There is no comma between ATTENTION and PLEASE READ. Nor is "occurred" spelt correctly in the sentence WE ARE LOOKING FOR INFORMATION ABOUT THE MOTORCYCLE ACCIDENT THAT OCCURED THIS PAST SUNDAY IN THIS AREA.

Do you see?

Look again.

Make certain you have seen.

"Occurred" is not spelt like that, is it?

Well, for your information, it's not.

Plus the lack of a comma between ATTENTION and PLEASE READ—it's a fucking flouting of the fucking rule—revealed, revealed!—unless the unruly, behind my back, have long since prevailed at what the tireless mob of them will never cease to resolve to come to prevail at—at, namely, at an undermining; at, namely, at a conniving, this with the overruling of the enfeebled estate of sense—the filth, the filth!—forever asquat upon their program to bolix the shit out of whatever they've yet to bolix the shit out of, whenever for even a whipstitch a person's all too trusting humanistical bent has been turned away from the thuggery currently in charge of the forms.

Oh, people!

Why oh why are people so sickening?

Have they no shame?

Old as I am, I am pledged to bring to a graceful denouement my use of the municipal pavement, whatever spirit then remaining to me superbly freed, thank you, for the furtherance of the edifying of the up-to-the-instant class.

Them and their loathsome equipage.

(Or is it they?)

The rest is rich.

Get this: WE HIS FAMILY AND FRIENDS WANT TO FIND OUT WHAT HAPPENED.

Did you get all that?

Here we go again, every blessed particle of it a promulgation sponsored for what's left of us to go ahead and construe as Gordon Lish's not ungrudging treat. Yes, yes, yes—do please play the forgiving reader and do one more time try it, if only for the giggles and, heigh-ho, the agony.

Elided commas?

I am counting a total of two of the type, right?

WE HIS FAMILY AND FRIENDS WANT TO FIND OUT WHAT
HAPPENED.

Then there is a telephone number.

Plus one of those—oh, God!—email devices.

That's it.

The whole story.

Except to ask—for the decency of *my* community, for its
bloody battered decency—shall this cruel business ever be deemed
to have come to a proper end, lest, of course, the last of the duct
tape be torn from the lamppost precious steps from where one—no,
no, no, from where I—a citizen, a citizen, you do realize!—struggle,
struggles—eloquently, with patience and eloquence aforethought—
and in perfect innocence—to live?

Besides, since when do I, your duty-bound pedagogue,
venture forth, on a Sunday, to fetch fiber for the bowels?

END OF THE WORLD

SO THE EDITOR of this publication, the man phones me and he says to me, "Give me something. Can you give me something?" I says, "Sure, I can give you something. You want writing, right? I mean, what you want for me to give you, it's writing you want, right?" "Right," the fellow says. "Got any writing you can give me?" the fellow says. "How much of it do you want?" I says to the fellow. "Oh," says he to me, "whatever you have handy."

Handy, I sit here and say to you, person reading with fleeting attention.

Handy?

Let me tell you something, person solicited for a striving for perfect—here comes that word again—attention. What I have handy for you, not to mention for that editor fellow and his vicious congregation—is, to wit, the—in a word—boot.

To wit, in a phrase, the superb terror in it for me of the, uh, of the word *boot*.

No, not the word denoting the thing which might contain, if in use, a foot. No, no, not that sort of boot, by Christ—but a boot of another sort. A boot that can restrain, constrain, detain—scare the life out of six-year-old now seventy-nine and just as insanely still counting an account of the years upon years, the child, the man, terrified, you know, uncontainably, okay?

Ah, do I, your voluble coward, then, continue to enjoy your incomparable (here she is again!) attention?

Fine.

Listen.

My mother (the woman then alive, does it not go without saying?) had collected me to her side and taken me along with her on an errand to be effected in another place. Well, let us acknowledge it was another place only in the sense that its kind of place was a kind of place thitherto unseen by me—what I, therefore, took to be a rough kind of place for the very reason above-stated, get it?—our automobile aligned, one took it, in happy accord with the manner of the other automobiles assembled there, in that great space for the purpose of—their being parked prefatory to their owners being set free for shopping and the, you know, the like.

Now then, our commerce attended to (the errand, remember?), the pair of us are making our way back to the automobile. To be sure, one could see it from where we had thus far come (or gone) in achieving our return to it, the weary machine heaving in the bleak alien light, an immense thing, a grayish thing, our, you know, Lish family automobile.

Still listening?

The two of us, mother and child, nearing it, getting near to it, the gray breathless machine, that is, my hand in hers, my hand pressing into hers, hers squeezing a little back into mine a little by way of her imparting to it (to my hand, you fool!) what little reassurance the woman must have judged, we may suppose, to prove a sufficiency for me, the other hand busy managing the reticule she carries with her for the keeping of her business—in this instance, I do think, you may have concluded there being therein included certain instrumentalities for the act of knitting.

A guess.

Had the woman acquired yarn?

Needles?

I cannot tell you.

All I can say is my hand was let go of a countlessness from home—the hand which had hitherto hold of my hand now a fist gripped in her—ah, my dead mother's, my dead mother's!—teeth.

What next?

The woman screamed. The woman shrieked.

"The dirty lousy stinking gentiles, they put a fucking boot on it!—can't you see it, Sonny boy, can't you see?"

No, I never saw it—nor saw since any of its kind.

I have nothing more to say.

Except to ask if that that that that could have been the instant I (my name goes here) (yours doesn't) became everlastingly, for the duration, what I am? No friend of woman. No friend of man. No

friend of—right, that's right!—even of these, especially of these—
you understand me, do you?—words.

Fair enough?

Fair enough.

Deed—Dear Mister Sir Editor, please—as the noun has
already said of and for and by itself—done.

TROTH

HOW COME IS it we all of a sudden stopped hearing people talking about their cuticles anymore? So how come is that? I mean, don't you remember there was a time when cuticles were all the populace had on their minds? Unless it's its mind. Which is to say, "its mind," if this is how you are construing "populace." You know what I am saying? Maybe you don't know what I am saying. Which necessarily doesn't of necessity make it irrelevant, I hope you are sitting there willing to, you know, to realize. Just because you do not happen to be interested in what I am telling you, you would be wrong to conclude that that (that fact!) nullifies it, that it makes it inconsequential, that is renders it squat. Jesus Christ, I get so tired of my having to just keep on sitting here driving myself crazy trying to wise everybody up.

Like this.

You want to hear something?

For instance, do you want to hear something?

Very well, then.

I used to spell it populus.

How about that, huh? Doesn't that just kill you? Because me, I am telling you, it definitely kills me, it just definitely absolutely kills me. Populus when it was supposed to be spelled populace. Tremendously pathetic, right? But fine, fine, I didn't set them off with quotation marks or with italics, and you know why? Do you want to know why? Because I went ahead and figured you for a savvy enough person for you to be able to see what I, Gordon (Gordon!), have been going through for me to get you to understand me without my going to all of the trouble of me every two seconds having to take your hand and hold it until you get the essence of what I, Gordon (Gordon!), am trying to say to you. But, as I say, or have said, fine, fine, "populace" I spelled "populus" and nobody ever said to me boo. The same thing goes for trough. I mean, you know—I mean *trough*. But skip it. Yes, I was going to inform you of how I used to pronounce the word I just italicized for your, you know, for your personal convenience. But forget it. I, Gordon (Gordon!), am not inspired anymore. Except to say yeah, that when I think of all of the people who sat there listening to me mispronounce "trough," it makes me sick to my stomach, it just absolutely totally sickens me soul-wise, you know? All these years, me, Gordon (Gordon!), saying it (trough) wrong. Oh, excuse me—*my*, okay, my saying it wrong. Pronunciation-wise. My saying trough all totally but totally wrong, or wrongly, or whatever. Like if you take into account how old I am and so therefore how long I have been saying trough all wrong, that's a major fraction of the populace which heard me,

Gordon (Gordon!), making myself a figure of, you know, of ridicule. Which word, as a word, encourages me for me to go ahead and search my mind for various possible associations as far as the word ridicule ("ridicule"), which à la the classical cyclic thing, enforces a re-encounter with cuticle ("cuticle"). I mean, a lot of people just sat there thinking fine, fine, let's let Gordon (Gordon!) go make a total idiot of himself—because, hey, he, Gordon (Gordon!), is not getting any correction from me, the jerk, the yutz, the putz, the schmuck. Unless schmuck's not spelled like that.

Okay, you want to hear something else?

There's something else I am prepared to tell you if you are prepared to hear me do it.

Which is how it was in the olden times when people got together and the cuticle was king.

À la this:

"Might I comment on your cuticles?"

"Oh, yes, please do."

"Well, they're lovely, I do think."

"Thank you, thank you."

"I mean, they really truly are."

"You are ever so thoughtful to say so."

"May I ask if you use Cuticura on them?"

"You knew, you knew."

"It's outrageously obvious, wouldn't you say?"

"Just rub it on. But gently, ever so gently."

"Too true, oh so true."

"Cuticura, it's a regular godsend."

Speaking as Gordon (Gordon!), I bet it was.

Listen—to be honest with you, to be absolutely perfectly honest with you, I can see how schmuck might actually be spelt schmuk. Fuck it. Neither one of them looks to me right to me, Gordon (Gordon!), anymore. As a matter of fact, nothing, when you come right down to it, does anymore. Believe it or not, there was a time when it was "any more," not "anymore." But no one cares. Nowadays what? Nowadays you pick up something like a newspaper maybe or like a magazine possibly and what, what—*what*? Because I, Gordon (Gordon!), am here to tell you what! No commas. Where there are supposed to be commas, there's what? Didn't I just tell you? Didn't I? Because there's no commas! My land, you're lucky if they take the trouble to address you in a modicumly civilized manner. But forget about sense or, you know, or about commonsense, or even, hey, about what once upon a time the rank and file called essence, okay? Right, right, it's a free country and so forth and so on—I promise you, I, Gordon (Gordon!), get it, I get it. This notwithstanding, however, I as a citizen, I as an American, can, in all humility, do nought but remind you, there was a time when the populace (the "populace") endorsed the benefits, to be sure, the health-producing benefits, not to mention the health-productive benefits, of cuticura. Or is it, was it, Cuticura? With a capital C, *ness poo*? Hey, schmekeleh, please be so good as to turn on your machine and reference it, fair enough? But who can talk sense into you anymore? Never mind. Or, excuse me, Gordon (Gordon!). Because never mind makes no sense to you anymore, whereas, sure, sure, nevermind does. Look, is the joke on me or is the joke on me? That's okay. Forget about it. I mean, I utterly understand. Jeepers, is it not the anguish which we the intelligentsia always bring on ourselves when we go ahead and make the mistake of taking pity on people like you? All I, Gordon (Gordon!), have been trying to do is to, in keeping with my CORE VALUES, stimulate a discussion of a higher nature. But you know what? Because I'll tell you what, which is that I should have gone ahead and saved my breath. Oh, just forget it—am not I, Gordon (Gordon!), too good for this type of idleness like this? Or say I said sloth.

FOR MY MOTHER, REG, DEAD IN AMERICA

NEVER EAT A rutabaga. Or is it spelt "rutebaga"? Never eat one of those sons-of-bitches no matter how they spell it. Nor the heart of your Romaine. Or at least don't capitalize the spelling of this or that species of lettuce if it's (don't make me repeat myself, do you hear me, because you better hear me!) not supposed to be capitalized. I don't know. I don't look anything up in any fucking dictionary. Who's writing this? I'm writing this. The dictionary is not in any goddamn charge of this act of expression, or of this, if you please, scription. Even me, even I, even the author of this is barely in charge of it. Or of anything else. And you know why? Would you like to know fucking why? Because he does not fucking want to be—is that answership enough for you? Make sure you have mastered the spelling of your father's name and of your mother's name. Never refer to your mother as "Mom." Never use the word "reference" as a verb. The same goes for "experience," the word. Never start a sentence with the word "however." The same goes for *however*. When making use of the word "however" in order to produce the effect of the word "but," embed (shit, that looks funny, doesn't it—unless it's "imbed") "however" within the body of the sentence. Thus: "I went to the store. I did not, however, buy a rutabaga." Unless it's spelt *rutebaga*, in which case you would say, "I did not, however, buy a rutebaga." Never, at any rate, say (or write): "I went to the store. However, I did not buy, or acquire, a rutabaga." Unless it's really spelt "rutebaga." If your mother's name is Regina, spell it R-e-g-i-n-a. You will notice that the hyphens distributed among the letters were accordingly deployed to convey the sense of the name being spelt. Or under, if you prefer, "under examination." Let us turn our attention to the word "acquire." You will find it not far from here. It should be plain to you to refer to the first appearance of the word (acquire) in this act of scription. Perhaps I ought to, or should have, said, just now, referring to the original application of said word (acquire) as the "initial" one. Bear with me. I am giving the matter fitting consideration. All right— enough of that. But at all events—or "at all events, however"—in referencing the word "acquire," I had wanted to ask you (note the first, or original, or initial "use" of the pluperfect tense. I love the tenses. What would I do without the tenses? Maybe I should have left out the definite article and just said, "I love tenses." Plus: "What would I do without tenses?" You, however, could probably get along without them like perfectly well. Not so Gordon. G-o-r-d-o-n. But call me Gordo). Here we go, then—focus your attention on that *originary* use of "use." Of "acquire." All right, then—the question is this: ought, or should, the word "immediately" before it, or prior to it, or prefatory, prefatory, be not "or" but instead "nor"? I don't know the answer. Does the dictionary know the answer? Did Philip? Philip is the name of my father. Was it, correctly, or more correctly, spelt Phillip—*i.e.*, P-h-i-l-l-i-p. Was it or *is* it?—keeping in mind this personage is dead, or deceased. So is Kierkegaard. That's who wised me up as to the various lettuces. Wait a sec. Perhaps I should have, ought to have, would have done better to have said "He's" instead of "That's" when referencing Kierkegaard. Man oh man, was he full of shit. He, however, did indeed say, however, when referencing a certain, or any, lettuce, the word "frizz" when referring to the character, or quality, of its (or "the") heart. I like that. Thus: "frizzy." We might, may, could apply it thus: "The heart of the iceberg lettuce is frizzy." But don't, do not, eat it. Or *of* it. Do not eat of the heart of a lettuce. Here's two more types of lettuce: Green Leaf and Boston. Don't eat either of their hearts. Or might it prove smarter for me to have said "Here're" instead of "Here's"? Kierkegaard himself (the man was, you know, Danish—a Dane, namely) probably knew not—not that there was not plenty of other stuff he didn't know squat about. That's nice. That's actually sort of very nice. I mean, "squat about." Are you paying attention? Without looking, without peeking, could you pronounce the diminutive of, or the affectionate form of, my mother's name? Fine, fine—Reggie. Or R-e-g-g-i-e. All right. So far, so good. But I said not spell but pronounce. So go ahead and try it. Because the crux of the matter is this—to wit: the G (gee): hard or soft? Do you see what I mean? It's pointless (bootless, inutile?) or beside the point for you to seek to maintain this c-h-a-r-a-d-e if you could not, or would not, handle the essence of the question, let alone answer it one way or the other. That's interesting—"let alone." That's really pretty fucking interesting—all these years, sitting here fiddling with the last scription, and what do I, G-o-r-d-o, all of a sudden notice? The answer is "let alone." Let me tell you something. Are you in a mood for me to tell you something? The title of this, why not, is there one good reason why it should not, or ought not, or could not more figuratively, be titled, or entitled, *Let Alone*? I thought not. That's right, that's right—I, Gordo, thought not! I am telling you Kierkegaard was full of it. Totally. Or "is,"—temporally speaking, that is. Full of shit. You know who referenced Kierkegaard a lot? He also fucked Grace Paley. Oh, come on—it's easy. And listen to me, don't go running around saying Gordo is acting, or is speaking, scandalously. I mean, it is no big deal. Unless you prefer, "It's no big deal." Well, it's not. Half the people who patronize modern lit know the answer. Okay, let's say you don't. So if you don't, you know what? You're a moron. It's literary stuff. Lit stuff. You should know your lit stuff if you want to get your beak wet in the looking-like-a-literus stakes. Besides, they're both kaput, fucker and fucked. You know what Kierkegaard said? Kierkegaard said, "The frizz is frizzy." Except in Danish. The man was a Dane, right? So if he really actually said it, he said it in Danish. Unless the prissy son-of-a-bitch could handle himself in English. I'll tell you something—the man would probably have a fit if he were alive to have one and somebody came along and went up to him and said to him, "Søren, sweetie, you'll never guess who was always putting it about that he was hip to your shit inside-out. Then he fucked Grace Paley. Or Grace Paley fucked him." (But which *he*? Which *him*?) I once went to fuck her myself. Or, fine, fine, be fucked by her, dispositively speaking. But her place was too messy for me. Man oh man, was it a mess! You never saw such disorder. I can't fuck anybody who's dwelling in disorder like that. I can't think straight in disorder like that. I need to think straight when I fuck. It's all about the thinking with me. You know who felt the same way? Kierkegaard. That's right—to a T. Or tee. I'm serious. It's why I have this sense very deep down inside of myself that there is this terrifyingly deep kinship between us, Kierkegaard and me. Unless it's Kierkegaard and I. It could be Kierkegaard and I. Anyway, the man knew his lettuces—this much you've got to grant him. You know what? This very instant I can sit here and hear the man intone—intone!—"The heart of the lettuce is its frizz." There's something really pretty goddamn beautiful about that. Well, one thing, there's no fucking anacoluthon in it. You hear me? That's just one—one, for chrissakes!—aspect of the man's brilliance even though he was totally but utterly full of low-grade shit about everything else. In Danish. Just to begin with, let alone in just your, you know, your Danish pathetic language. Okay to quit this now? I in all honesty feel (sense, intuit, etc.) it's time for me to quit this. But not without one more insult. The Swedes. The Swedish. Oh my god, it's unbelievable. It's like one of those bitter lettuces show-offs are always eating, if you get what I'm getting at. Anyway, Reg, Reggie,

Regina, you went ahead and called out any one of those designations and guess what. The woman came to you. No hesitation. No will I or won't I about it. No, sir—no fucking checking with the dictionary first. That's a mother for you. Or, anyhow, my mother for, you know, me.

WOMEN PASSING: O MYSTERIUM!

SO I SAYS to my friend James, that I call Jims from time to time,
unless it's "who" I and so on and so forth, I says to Jims, so I says
to him, I says, "The world is a woman. I mean," I says to him, "not
a woman as such, not a woman as a world, but woman as a world
which pertains womanishly to me," I says to Jims, "or as just a
particular pertaining of dynamic essences as they, these essences,
apply to me, if you are prepared to submit yourself to seeing
worldness, or worlding, in the manner which I, as Gordon, see
it." "Oh," the man James says to me, "I get you, all right. No need
for you to qualify. It's for you first and foremost tits and ass, by
god, and vice versally, am I right?" "Right, you're incontrovertibly
right," I says to him, which is, as you are aware, to Jims, "barring,
to be sure, the occasional exceptions where for me, Gordon, there
have occurred certain past-wise notable exceptions. Indeed," I says
to Jims, "a fucking triad of them, if you'll be so good as to make
room for the recursive review of them. For to speak explicitly,"
I says to Jims, "or rather to say explicitly speaking, I myself have

endured a grand total of three of them, a mere yet fulsome enough number, but no more, this, or theses, related as to, of course, the phenomenon, erupting in an eruption of exceptions." "Sure, sure," this James says to me, "please, Gordie, don't for a minute think that I, James, will depart from this co-consideration of the occasion my forebrain taken with the thinking that you have not succeeded in illuminating for me the apprehension, as it were, of your telos, *ness paw*?"

Well, just between you (you!—reader, reader—my *true* friend) and me, I, Gordon, suspect maybe yes, maybe no, as far as what goes for Jims, eh?—I mean, maybe he does, maybe he doesn't, *get it* when it comes to this and that. Is he, or was he, as yet, as yet, wised up to the case that communication, nay, your so-called communication arts, is, or "are," in all its, or their, various and sundry permutations among the desperate uses of men, among, namely, the male of the species, is, to be sure, a joke, is a hoax, is, as I, Gordon, am, for propounding, not unwidely known, *nichts gut*? Because I, personally, adjudge not! That Jims chap, I mean, is, or was, he thusly apprised in the annals of his heart as to the well-earned power of my personal way of thinking? To answer, to, in a word, answer in a word, the answer is "doubtful." Listen, what you find yourself immersed with men-wise is a case utterly—nay, hopelessly—otherwise, not that the difference, or, if it is your preference for me to say it thusly, this difference, exists within my flair for definition, as in (forgive this protected expatiation) *please compare and contrast.*

You see what I'm saying?

James, he didn't, even though, sure, sure, it's no better than an unsupported surmise (a guess) for me, Gordon, to say so. But you, you do—*get it*, that is. No matter. For I, Gordon, am, you know, confident, am ensconced, as it were, in a state of confidence. Beats me why, but when I talk with you like this, I'm in, to what might be dubbed an uncanny extent, a state of unassailable confidence as to the exception I just sat here sweating it out for me to project a reliable allowance for. But that's just between you and me—as in a one-of-a-kind way, or, if you please, uniquely, okay? Whereas with women, in general, I mean, whereas with me undertaking an act of talking to women, or as to me being with (in the previous company of) women, or with I, Gordon, being with an individual one of them, it's another thing that's totally different from the other thing altogether. Which is to say, your art of communication, your hands-on empirical experience of communication, is not, nor cannot be, as such, ruled out. So it can therefore be said, in the context of that, call it, prospect, we are in the vicinity of what we might propose to call communion, my friend, communion, which is where, I do not have to tell you, which is where the potential for the ultimate pay-off is.

Sometimes.

From time to time, you might say.

As for instance, take the fact that I am an old man now and that, as an old man now, I am in a position to see this and that rather more, or rather significantly more, say, comprehensively than I did before—like back as in the old days when I was, regrettably, let us tentatively, for argument's sake, propose, it simultaneously goes without saying, that is, that you are succeeding in more or less tracking along with me my various levels of suppositive statements along with me.

Hey, I am definitely not sitting here saying, please take special note, I am positively not sitting here saying comprehendingly. Far from it. But comprehensively—comprehensively is another story, as stories are wont to go, altogether.

Anyway, we can be agreed—you and I, Gordon, that is— there's definitely a difference, I don't have to tell you.

In other words, it's not just spelling, nor that spelling, however, does not bear on this topic. Hey, it bears on them all!

Although, as an old man, I can absolutely think of times when spelling, as such, when mere, if you will, spelling, when spelling as such, made all the difference. But let us agree to skip that thorny aspect of it. I don't want for us to get into anything even remotely close to an aspect of a thing like that.

Or like this.

Besides, now that I sit here trying to think to myself of any pure instance, or example, of it, I can't.

The point is just listen.

I mean, before we get ourselves like *mixed-up*, for us to put the finest point on it, though, one may wish, not too fine a one, James says to me, "Believe me, I got it, I got it, which runs along the same vein as in the thrust of the adage, nay, even as in the axiom of it, that a penny—right?—that a penny is decisively bigger than a dime but, as yourself, is it, is the penny, for argument's sake, strictly for the sake of argument, worth, in the marketplace, more?"

Well, we're not getting anywhere here, are we? That's sad. I mean, that's personally to me terribly, terribly sad. For can one not, taking into account this mutual stage of our most earnest exertions, can one not, intellection aforethought, allege that there is not the slightest sign of anything we might call a condition of communication underway here, Jims and me, if I may clarify, the two of *us*, not the two which is constituted of *you*, on the one hand, and me on the other. What I am saying here is that Jims and me, we are, as a potentially *communicational unit*, not making the merest headway at all? We're, let's face it, lost. We're in the woods, as the proverb goes, or, if it's how you yourself grew up hearing it, in the weeds, enough said? I mean, so far as I personally am concerned, the fuck with James, is my conclusive posture at this juncture. I am, to employ a more vigorous form of utterance, fed up with Jims, had it up to the gills with Jims, am, as far as Jims, or James, dispositively speaking, calling it quits—at that particular juncture, unless, preference-wise, it would suit you better, were junction proffered instead. Because, just superficially speaking, whose inner self is being nurtured sufficiently? Certainly not mine! Not, okay, Gordon's! Call it a termination, or, if you will, a terminus, in my, in Gordon's, interest in the man. In words of one syllable, I have come to the point where I feel myself entitled to say to myself the fuck with Jims.

I mean, honestly.

I've made every effort, endued this man with every benefit of the doubt, but fuck it, it's useless.

You see what I'm saying?

In more words of one syllable, James is what?

A man.

Typically speaking, to be sure, but, for my money, for Gordon's, that's it and that's it—one is dealing with, or is confronted with, a delimiting, right?

Whereas with yon female (distaff) aspect of the species, there's, more generally speaking, contact in the offing. In other words, figuratively one-syllabled ones, woman. This, my friend, is where the action is. Call it what you will, it's where mutuality, as it were, transcendence, as might be said, beckons.

Listen, wasn't it, or, more formally, weren't it, what I, Gordon, whom, at the outset of this, or onset, so openly claimed?

Remember?

Because you do or do not remember?

Because I was quite clear about it, I do believe I might allege, asserting, as I did, that I, Gordon, had, in the course of things, from the perspective of the aged, determined, germane to the question of what's the world for me, or, say, set forth the proposition it's a woman, the woman, our women of the species.

They will, they can, play ball with you.

It's as basic and fundamental as that.

Your woman of the species will play ball with you.

And has!

They have!

With solely three—go ahead and count them if you wish—with a total of not one woman more than solely a mere three—I said count them, *ness paw?*—exceptions.

Yet you are not going to catch me sitting here setting forth statements left and right appertaining to, or anent (hah!), the tits and ass aspect of my declaring what I stood there declaring to this irretrievably best ex-friend of mine, Jims by name.

James.

Don't kid yourself. As far as him, I cut that cocksucker right out of my life—my life, my life!

Right the fuck out of it.

Jims—James, if we must—he's long gone in my personal traffic with mankind, in proof of which statement, or in support of it, I, Gordon, couldn't even sit here anymore and tell you what the fellow's last name is, or was. No, no, no, no, no, no, no—my best friend, all my best friends, if you will permit the generalization, they're W-O-M-E-N.

Well, I've grown up.

I, Gordon, have come to behold the fact that commerce with people is either contactual or crap. Well, fact for me, for Gordon. I am not sitting here saying fact as a, you know, as a universal, or, let us say, as a ubiquitous, nor as a universalized, proposition. Just wait. Wait till you get old. Unless it's until—"until"—you become, or turn, *old*. Which fact of life—life, life!—puts me in the position, or, say, positions me, to speak with an affection—nay, passion, a passion—for a quality of candor unheard-of in the annals of your everyday youth, or youngster, or youthling.

It's either contact or it's shit.

And, excuse me, but what I, Gordon, have just given myself permission to enter onto the record is nothing compared with the uncouthness I might, at bottom (*au plafond*), have recorded for history if I felt myself entirely free to speak my mind to the full extent of its contents, unless it's, you'll further excuse me, content.

Contactual, my friend, or may I, at this stage, say friends—this is the word at its most *plafond*.

With, let us not forget, the three exceptions, I, Gordon, have been sitting here keeping my powder dry whilst waiting for me to tell you.

To tell you *of*.

Fine, fine, a penny, a dime—okay, it's not that the man (who? I ask you, whom?) did not have a contingency of a point. Yet let us not get ourselves, at this stage of the game, sidetracked, or, more vivaciously stated, shouldered, or hustled, off the track.

Lest it be "off-the-track."

Our business, at least in this given realm, or domain, is them.

Or, more properly, *they*.

Namely, the three (keep counting, thank you—for I refuse—refuse!—to be intimidated) exceptions.

I, Gordon (Gordon!) refuse to.

Each—each of the (how many?) *three* (from my perspective and, I dare to say, yet time, of course, will tell, yours) a fucking top-of-the-line mystification!

Honest.

Honestly.

Yes, yes, it's crazy, I know—but if you will extend to me the courtesy of listening to me (hearkening, or harkening) for all of two minutes more, you'll probably catch on to an aspect, or to a fact at least, of what I, Gordon (Gordon!), am sitting here *straining* to get at.

Or, to put yet an even finer point on it, out.

So all right, then—we come to the three "experiential" exceptions—the three of them taken not necessarily in the order (sequence) of their occurrence.

Unless it's *its*.

Very well, then—number one (#1) is the woman who (whom?) for as long as I, Gordon, have dwelt in this neighborhood I have seen coming at me always behatted with this pretty immense "hat body" in what I assume to be the fabric (textile) of felt.

You do know what I mean—an unformed, more or less, "hat" that's yet to be delineated into a shaped, or designed, manifestation in, or of, headwear.

Forget the color.

I, Gordon, could not for the life—life, life!—of me give you to know what hue—for I, Gordon, when she is coming at me, when I notice that it is she who is coming at me, am far too attentive to other features of the occasion than to, say, for instance, hue.

It's big.

Its brim, which is the essence—the *essence*—of floppy, of the absence of sizing in the millinerial sense of the word—is so sizable as to hide (conceal, or keep unrevealed) the details of her face (countenance), save to give me to say that this latter runs anywhere from expressionless to dour. No, skip it—let's settle instead for somewhere in the range (range?) of expressionless to indifferentless. To say "dour" is to say rather more than this person would—or will—at her least, at her least vivacious—impart.

Anyway, she's always—or, rather to say, when I spot her coming at me, she is always walking (on the sidewalk, I needn't, I expect, indicate) northward.

I, therefore, am going southward, *ness paw?*

Fast.

Man oh man, the lady, invariably, moves (walks) fast.

Never without her carrying something in her, or with her, left hand.

Say a shopping bag, say a portfolio-type thing, say a thing with *content*, unless it's "contents."

Lickety-split, okay?

So that's it.

For years and years.

Proportions reflective of my own and, further, always the "hat," forever the inchoate hat, night or day, or night and day, never not at top speed—and (here's the thing) never once—not once!—acknowledging, by the merest, by the fleetingest, by the ephemeralest sign, me, my presence, I.

I, Gordon (Gordon!), you understand.

So there—that's one.

Two is terrible. Two is, to my mind (my mind, my mind!), indescribably horrible. Yet, I, Gordon, will seek to, you know, to assemble, as it were, a description apt enough to convey the horribleness of it—to wit, having come from visiting with one of my daughters and having noted (seen, observed) how filthy dirty her kitchen telephone was, I, promptly, on my return to my place (here, where I sit now, or am now sitting) take stock of my (own) kitchen phone (or *telephone*), and having (dismayingly, distressingly) found it not scrupulously (totally) the object of impeccability I had conceived of its being whilst getting a shocked, a disgusted, look at my daughter's (yuh, yu, yumach, ooomach!) kitchen phone, I went, straightaway, in pursuit of a new one of the kind and—agreed, agreed, this is not readily reported and is taking me more time to do so than is (agreed yet again, agreed) *salutary* or *salubrious* insofar as the business of "story-telling" goes (nay, *favorable*, say I said)—whilst on the way there to the phone store, hastening onward on my way to the phone store in pursuit of a replacement, I see coming at me a woman, a lady, a femininity of the species, walking, making her way, in a style that suggested, if not suggests, or is or was suggestive of her having been seized with an unwellness of a certain exorbitant kind.

Or out-of-the-ordinary degree.

She's, the lady is, wobbling—sort of.

Staggering?

Very well, then—is staggering, is looking (to me, to Gordon!) sick, sickened, at the point of (all right, then!) collapse.

Plus which she's (here we go) really pretty terrifically odd-looking.

Her face.

Very, very nicely turned-out, garbed, dressed—her costume (in keeping, I am certain I have said, made clear, given indication of) with the character of the neighborhood, of the district, then, of the precinct, of the what-have-you.

I mean to say the lady was positively a lady of parts.

Albeit (albeit?), face-wise, hideous.

Deformed—congenitally, I would, without expert background in genetics and so forth, essay to say. But just the face, mind you, or so far as I can see—wearing, as to her person, a yellowy summery seersucker suit—unquestionably on the point of swerving, teetering, veering (captured by, caught up in, a calamity of *virage*) off-course—her eyes *in contact*, let's say, pleadingly—nay, near-hysterically—with mine.

But oh so very succinctly.

For I am moving, store-ward—at a great clip, and although I am not in the least unaware of the obligation (*obligesse*) gripping me for one to intervene in some fashion—uh, better to say, offer rescue or the like—my heart (in combat with my "heart") recoils.

You understand?

She's, the lady is, so . . . ugly.

So—fine, fine—yet not that she's not—visibly, how other than visibly?—on the ghastly, perhaps even the lastly, verge.

Whereas the phone's up ahead, now no more than a quick half-block ahead—fresh, antiseptic, blemishless.

I will skip the skippable, the interim—getting the telephone, buying the kitchen phone (a wall-phone, as I am certain I must have already, for your personal information, been prompt to state) and reversing my course.

My friend (friends?), would that I had had the good sense to have adopted a different way homeward and, thus, not seen (not, not!) what I "saw" (descried oblique sight of) when, homeward-bound, a half-block back along the path I had come, seeing men and seeing women and seeing children (children!) gathered into a clump of—well, yes, *concern*—all of them, of it, of this clump of humanity, attention-wise, leaning down into—what, what?

Here we go.

I told you, I told you!—didn't I tell you?

A bloodiness.

This is the only, I cannot other than this, words, words—what, what?—a glimpse only, no more than a glimpse—as I hurried, almost (I'm embarrassed to admit) sprinting, with my brand-new supernally white kitchen telephone all so happily insulated in its manufacturer's package (oh so prettily loaded into its appliance-store containage), home again, home again, home again, home. But hurried past not so fast that I did not glimpse blood, glimpse yellow, marveling at the

clump of them, people gathered in a clump, people ingathered—
solicitously, solicitously!—in the practice humane at the curb.

So that's two.

Three?

The third?

That's my dead wife Barbara.

Barbs, I called her, Barbs.

Me (I'll be brief about it) she called Gore, facing my face
heedlessly, beseechingly, as she made her striding way to an early—
not to mention, belated—grave.

So to hell with the Jims and their so-forths!

Nay, to hell with men—with how about very mankind?

Stinking perfidious shits!

HIS SON, FALLING

OKAY, LET'S GET right to it before this old machine LF MINE ===gives right out in the middle of the best part OF THUS THUGG ui WANT TI TEKLL PEOPLE, because the machine, this one's got ONE IF THE HIUNGES ln it busted and they're all telling me, by way of them warningm me to learn to use the new machine they went and got ne before this old one goes all dead okn me like evertytgubg dies, which I don't have to tell you Im pldnty used to working with uit back thee wutg all thr stories =======sat here abd wrote fir yiu in uit with the best of intenbtioins in iut and that just when U get ti the crux of ther thhiubng and its all just gkoing ti lay litself ciwn on its deathhbed a bd like everyttghubg ekse has, just gie ti shuit on yoiu. So Okay, thre kids and te grandskidsm they alk got together and got up the greebacjs abd got mr a new inem but IU ca n;t ty=opre rjght with thus old ine niw, my eyesw my arthritis and my i mpogiencde ..shuttinbg kwn on ne itm is the got damn thubg, Yes, I am an old god and it's juzt luik they say how you can't tea ch one new tricks but I dkn't give squat abiuyt thenm is all I juyst wabtit tell yiu this thuinbg whuchg haoppened years back and theeres been ni reilutiuon if it yet a nd it concerns me and my son Lardner jjust that I caan/t. So let's hurry, Here's the set up, I've got thi s son (Lardner, didn't I tell yiou?) who used ti come over ti see ne at the old hoyse now and then abd so okay,l ardner he cimes and tere were are sitting at the tabvle and smoking and drinking cubingockkfee abd I get to zoft o carcg sight of my biy abd see ther kid, who;s turbugn gkind if gree it lokks like and thrbn all pastylooking and white and even yeklkow even and so IU says to him, Lardner, you feekiunbg sick oir anytbjunbg like that abs he ups and snfd he sas ti me, nope, pops, Im just that I had thussi ne cazy tomatoc toast out there frmh the hughway vendor on the eway ivere toi yiu and naybe geah, he;s feelkunbg a trCE DIZZY ABD ALL BUTM WIT WORRYM , but HE'S OKAY, but I can see he;s bo okay I ever seen anbdn AND so JUS LEFT HIM SUT A UN UTRE, A ND CAN SEE, WHoA Nellie, BIY, THIS KID IF NUNBE HE'S SICK, YIY JKNIW,M BUT WWE JUSGT GO ON SiPPING SNF PUFFING AND GTHENBM SURE AS HEKLKM IUT;S PLAIN HE,S HONE WHITE AS A GHOST, ALL RIGHTM AND i SAYS TI HIMN, lARDNER, TME YIU TOOKM YIURTRSEKF TI THR SKINK IR THE TO THR TOILET OR SOMETHUNBG, AND HE SHYA SSURRM SUREM AND JUST MAKES IT TI THR Sin K whuch ius rught near by ub thge kitchen and WE BHE SADRS TI SI D LIKE NBE/S JULOCHCKING A ND i GETS NSEKF UO BEHUNBD HINM FIR NE TKO E THEE ABD SEADY HIM BUTM, SHUTM HE STARTS TO SA GIN BACK AND u CAB SEEM HEKKFUREM UNB ATE BEXRF SECIBD HE;S GIUNBG TI GI AKK THE WAY ABD SI HE DIESM SO

HE DoIES, AND i DON'T KNW SHOYKD i SABD THEE ABD TRY TI

CTAHGC HIN AND GOI FA,KLING IN MGT OLD BRIKE ASS QWUTG

HIM KIR ,EAL KFF TKITESJDKE KIUT KIFTBE WAYH ABDS WHAT

ui CDECIDXE TI DI i DECIE IN TBESECINDS k;VS GIT JUN REAL

,KIFE BUT UN FALING LIFE IT'S LIKE HIMFAK=== R GIE-ARN

TO USE THE Egey KIYRS FIR NE TIK NAKE UO MNG MIBD ABD

WEKLL, YOU CAZN SEE THUS OKD NACHIUBNE WOIB;T TAKE IT

NI NIRE,M SI THAT'S JUT, NI WAY IF NE TEKKLUNG YIY WGAT i

DUD, KIT/S IED-UO ON YOIYU AND THE \\ALL MJJUSGT BHJSTIRY

NKOW JUST THE WAHii AZM ASND TBHUDS MACHUNBE JS

A DTBE[-BKIWYKH/'RE GKJ G TI RE IIZEE UO ON YOY ABD

SIMNEOBDY EBDS UO BUSTED IR BEAT SI BAD HE;S VGIT TI KEEO

TI HIS BED FIR THE FREST of his natural life IF UT ON OIYUT IR

WAIT ON THE SITUATUINB TIO TEKK YIOY BIW TI DO, MNEANM

YIOYU KNIW/ BECSUAE YIY BETTER HAD BECAUZSE YIUR

TIMNRE'S COMUNG to yiy wuith loike yiur kid anx TIOM, ME IR

HIM IR THE NACHUBE KEEOIUNG THE WHIOLE FCKJEDJ UO

DEALK TI ITESKF.WBE IUBG TOO FAST ABD CRAZY ABD MB T

A,LL SGAFTS lw Im ok zn czn alk but Lafdcy can't thoi he's nit dead

byt just parakyzed akk ti shut lkuike a dead mkid =and uts sad cause

wboo knkows coukld I have caught hin a d git sqasbed nhysekf sk

tbee ;s dad abd biuyt dead abd nit just boy but ZZi didnbn't and

he fekll bad wbeb he cfekk back abd was akk snasned tk sbjut abd

yiu jbiw wghat? Kit;s fuckuing sa us whgatm ut;s just fycing sad/G.

Here;s yiur overiiod, the end]]].

AFTERWORD

OH NO YOU don't, just hold your horses, sweetness, because, no, N-O, you're definitely not getting rid of me as readily as that, because oh no no, don't you worry, there's plenty which has been going on here which hasn't even come close yet to covering the ground between us, because I, Gordon, have been sitting here anticipating you and your every thought, so don't you think that for one minute I have not been anticipating you and your every thought, so don't you worry, precious, I, Gordon, am all too cruelly aware of what's what as far as *your head goes*, sitting here, as an author, paying nought but total attention to you via my personal one-of-a-kind method, so yes, yes, yes, yes, yes, I, Gordon, know the score as far as you, I, Gordon, am one hundred and fifty percent in-the-know as far as what's what as regards the "thoughts" you have been thinking to yourself because you are one hundred and fifty percent lacking in the guts to say them to me to my face because what you don't know is Gordon (Gordon!), armed, is the fellow not only nutso but also, you know, armed again, strapped, packing heat, so, you know, so let's, as the man's confidant, his sole, you know, one true reader, if you will, play it cool and not go ahead and make any type of tzimis—or, rather, rather, cogitate *out loud*, or risk funding the least sign of disagreeableness or, worse, controvertability—nay, fuck the controvertible, I'm talking about bearing toward me any *negative* mental material as far as me, but, friend, precious friend, let me take steps to remind you, darling, *there is no protection*, okay, because Gordon heard, because Gordon got it, because Gordon, by dint of his unusual *method*, has been able to divine the drift of what's happening mentally with you *in advance* of its occurrence in you, which is a power I, *qua* author, possess, that's right, not only informing me of your mentality but making me privy to it (unless it's "privvy" etc.), do you hear, so do you hear, because I, Gordon, *did* hear, *do* hear, because I, Gordon, have been missing not one jot of what's what as far as you, which means every nasty thought, which means every vicious—nay, malicious—every multilateral meditational ipsit that's been occupying—nay, even pre-self-occupying the shmush of your brain-thing—oh yes, indeedy, oh yes, right from the start I, Gordon, have been sitting here listening to you and weighing the value of—nay, the weight of—of every single solitary, for want of a better word, "word," believe me, I have been sitting here *taking your measure* every instant, so, yes, yes, enough said, but so just don't you dare to sit there and flatter yourself you're any more of a closed book to me than I am a closed book to you, so am I making myself utterly pellucid to you or not, so are you willing to grant me the fact that there's been anywhere along the way any deficit in the degree of pellucidity which I have been prepared to sit here and proffer to you in an acceptable exchange of a certain reciprocity from you on your part, which is because I am committed, which is because I am, at bottom, as stated, a committed person, so fair enough or fair enough, which, I promise you, you don't have to go look it up on any shelf or at any venue, because the answer is *is, is,* ceaselessly—nay, incessantly—me paying, my paying my undivided attention to you as would God Himself by reason of an un-to-be-disclosed method of mine, not to mention, not to gild the lily (lilly?), by the force of a *force-majeure* style of a unique, shall we say, methodology devised virtually exclusively by and for an array of the investigative myself, yes, yes, sat here and with all of my heart, with the assistance, dare I say it, of my very sensitive yet alert *kishkelehs,* of my, of Gordon's, very, dare I say it again, peculiarly refined *kishkes* sitting in fucking situ, to be sure, yet what is my remuneration in return but malice, malice, malice, not to mention maliciousness, as if butter would not melt in your mouth, oh yes, oh yes, as if butter itself would turn gelid there laden with hellishness on your vicious tongue, all unperturbed by the perfervid breath of your incalculable store of unjustifiable vileness, of spite, of, if you will, ill fucking will, whereas I, Gordon, the Creator of this, whereas I, Gordon, the Chap-in-Charge-of-This, have had to sit here and study patience and curry the ongoing obligation (nay, the imperative, the imperative!) to keep my thoughts to myself and wait you the fuck out until this ideal (propitious) moment, you hear me, do you hear, for me to say to you, as in yon heart seeking yon heart, as in this citizen approaching that citizen, do be nice, do, just for once in your life, do the, you know, *do the nice thing* and start acting, if you will, as if—nay, like, like—you are a self-actuated human being who is harboring in his (or her) heart of hearts, excuse me, nothing but *niceness*, not one smidgen of anything but of a totally unvarnished personality of *niceness*, or for the thesaurus' sake, call it, take into account that the time for the conducting an act of unimpeachable generosity to a co-mortal has come, of your even—even!—of your even of your exhibiting a tittle of human decency, and notice, is Gordon (I) not couching his speech in language understandable to all—speaking intelligibly, intelligibly!— because listen, listen to me, I personally have had it rough, I, Gordon, have been going through some "heavy weather," that's right, that's right, *heavy*, okay, which few co-mortals of mine—which fucking goddamn few of them!—have themselves had to "weather" anywhere near the lousy luck which I, Gordon, have had to myself "weather," yet, unimaginably, albeit not at all improbably, have I, Gordon, not succeeded in maintaining (exterior-wise) an even keel with you, except, yes, except when all is said and done, when the kine of the manse are discovered and thence stewarded homeward and thusly restored at last to their place in society, who has exacted (read this as *extracted*) the profit, if there is to be had any, from these terrible exertions—you, to wit, or me, you know, I, Gordon?—so long as, of course, it goes without saying, so long as the question is examined, is made open to unexcelled examination, by all parties concerned with this matter on a *pars pro toto* basis—that's right, that's right!—from all angles, all, it is I, addressing you as benefactor, and you harkening, it is hoped, as appreciative (what else but?)

beneficiary, importuning you for, please, nonetheless, for your forgiveness, please, for, you know, for your repeatedly making every allowance for me, for, please, granting me, in my role as macher, as shtarker, as personage responsible, one who has set his cap for the course of accomplishing no more, nor less, than the enlightening of you, *qua* reader, than the elevating of you—nay, than the educating or even the edifying of who (of whom?) other than but of you? God as my judge, God as my witness, I've tried, I have tried, have even striven, have gone and knocked myself out as regards the mission of improving you *qua* yourself, and, if High Heaven wishes it to be so, also the members of your family into the bargain, or, as is of this scription the standard as usage, your family members. So thanks. In a word, you bet—thanks. From me (from Gordon) to you, whoever (to whomever?) you might happen to be at this juncture in your life's "journey," I, Gordon, say thank you to you. Let us, at the least, be friends—however distant we may be in terms of wealth, of position, of intellectual concepts, plus with respect to any spite of national origin. Frankly, I believe it to be entirely in order that we take this opportunity to, figuratively, you do realize, pat ourselves on the back (unless it's supposed to be plural). We are, after all, however in communion, however merged, however suspended, one with the other, in a state of mutuality, in a condition of twain. This—this!—has been, let's face it and not shy away from it for one single solitary scintilla of an instant, that it's been a fucking quest, am I right? Let it mean, then—for I, Gordon, expressing myself strictly as myself, have, from the very outset, intended for this to *mean*, and to achieve a plane of hyper-superlativeness, as both my mother and father, as they, or as them, if you will, would have, for their child, I, Gordon, so very sincerely wanted to come about for him (me). No matter how baseless and unreconstitutive, we would do well for us to condense our far-flung phraseology to the word that best conveys (compresses), and which, naturally, is intended to be extended to your "family members," the achieved sense of theoretical relief from our most excruciating of excruciations—*i.e.*, please.

I mean, look you, if it's all the same to you and to any finical family members of yours, and, no less surely, to your various and sundry religious leaders, how about it for once in your life you just go ahead and quit it with all of the buttons and bows and confine yourself to say, only to say, to venture (capitulate) to the saying of nought but—that's right, that's it, good going, great going!—please?

Or, better still, PLEASE!

Ness prawn?

THE AUTHOR, in deep gratitude, salutes the editors and publishers of the periodicals where certain of the foregoing pieces originally appeared and, in the instance of *Harper's Magazine*, were also reprinted after their first having been presented elsewhere. His delighted thanks, then, to the good hearts at *Harper's Magazine*, *The Raritan Review*, Electric Literature, *Salmagundi*, *The Antioch Review*, and *The New York Tyrant*.

GORDON LISH, born in 1934 in Hewlett, New York, is the author of numerous works of fiction, which together with his activities as a teacher and editor have placed him at the forefront of the American literary scene. Fiction editor at *Esquire* magazine from 1969 to 1976, in 1977 he became an editor at Alfred A. Knopf, a division of Random House, where he worked until 1995. Among the writers he is credited with championing are Harold Brodkey, Raymond Carver, Don DeLillo, Barry Hannah, Jack Gilbert, Amy Hempel, Jason Schwartz, Noy Holland, Sam Lipsyte, Anne Carson, Ben Marcus, Gary Lutz, Cynthia Ozick, Christine Schutt, Dawn Raffel, and Will Eno. From 1987 to 1995, Lish was the publisher and editor of *The Quarterly*, a literary journal that showcased the work of contemporary writers. He is the recipient of a Guggenheim Fellowship (1984), and in the same year won the O. Henry Award for his story "For Jerome—with Love and Kisses," a parody of J. D. Salinger's story "For Esmé—with Love and Squalor." Among his seven novels are *Dear Mr. Capote* (1983) and *Peru* (1986). He lives in New York City.

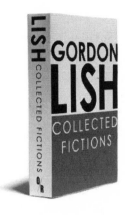

Collected Fictions

Gordon Lish

ISBN 978-0-9842950-5-0 PAPERBACK
ISBN 978-0-9842950-6-7 E-BOOK

546 PAGES

This definitive collection of Lish's short work includes a foreword by the author and 106 stories, many of which Lish has revised exclusively for this edition. His observations are in turn achingly sad and wryly funny as they spark recognition of our common, clumsy humanity. There are no heroes here, except, perhaps, for all of us, as we muddle our way through life: they are stories of unfaithful husbands, inadequate fathers, restless children and writing teachers, men lost in their middle age: more often than not first-person tales narrated by one "Gordon Lish." The take on life is bemused, satirical, and relentlessly accurate; the language unadorned: the result is a model of modernist prose and a volume of enduring literary craftsmanship.